MAPPO, THE MERRY MONKEY

RICHARD BARNUM

Edition : Culturea (Hérault, 34)
Contact : infos@culturea.fr
Print in Germany by Books on Demand
Design and layout : Derek Murphy
Layout : Reedsy (https://reedsy.com/)
ISBN : 9791041819782
Légal deposit : July 2023

MAPPO, THE MERRY MONKEY

CHAPTER I

MAPPO AND THE COCOANUT

Once upon a time, not so very many years ago, there lived in a tree, in a big woods, a little monkey boy. It was in a far-off country, where this little monkey lived, so far that you would have to travel many days in the steam cars, and in a steamship, to get there.

The name of the little monkey boy was Mappo, and he had two brothers and two sisters, and also a papa and a mamma. One sister was named Choo, and the other Chaa, and one brother was called Jacko, and the other Bumpo. They were funny names, but then, you see, monkeys are funny little creatures, anyhow, and have to be called by funny names, or things would not come out right.

Mappo was the oldest of the monkey children, and he was the smartest. Perhaps that was why he had so many adventures. And I am going to tell you some of the wonderful things that happened to Mappo, while he lived in the big woods, and afterwards, when he was caught by a hunter, and sent off to live in a circus.

But we will begin at the beginning, if you please.

Mappo, as I have said, lived in a tree in the woods. Now it might seem funny for you to live in a tree, but it came very natural to Mappo. Lots of creatures live in trees. There are birds, and squirrels, and katydids. Of course they do not stay in the trees all the time, any more than you boys and girls stay in your houses all the while. They go down on the ground to play, occasionally.

"But you will find the safest place for you is the tree," said Mappo's mother to him one day, when he had been playing down on the ground with his brothers and sisters. And, while they were down playing a game, something like your game of tag, all of a sudden along came a big striped tiger, with long teeth.

"Run! Run fast! Everybody run!" yelled Mappo, in the queer, chattering language monkeys use.

His brothers and sisters scrambled up into the tree where their house was, and Mappo scrambled up after them. He was almost too late, for the tiger nearly caught Mappo by the tail. But the little monkey boy managed to get out of the way, and then he sat down on a branch in front of the tree house where he lived.

"That wasn't very nice of that tiger to chase us!" said Mappo, when he could get his breath.

"No, indeed," said Mrs. Monkey. "Tigers are not often nice. After this you children had better stay in the tree—until you are a little larger, at least."

"But it's more fun on the ground," said Mappo.

"That may be," said Mrs. Monkey, as she looked down through the branches to see if the tiger were still waiting to catch one of her little ones. "But, Mappo, you and your brothers and sisters can run much better and faster in a tree than on the ground," said Mrs. Monkey.

And this is so. A monkey can get over the ground pretty fast on his four legs, as you can easily tell if you have ever watched a hand-organ monkey. But they can travel much faster up in the trees. For there is a hand on the end of each monkey's four limbs, and his curly tail is as good as another hand for grasping branches. So you see a monkey really has five hands with which to help himself along in the trees, and that is why he can swing himself along so swiftly, from one branch to another.

That is why it is safer for monkeys to be up in a tree than on the ground. There are very few other animals that can catch monkeys, once the five-handed creatures are up among the leaves. And monkeys can travel a long way through the forest without ever coming down to the ground. They swing themselves along from one tree to another, for miles and miles through the forest.

"Is it safe to go down now, Mamma?" asked Mappo of his mother, in monkey talk. This was a little while after the scare.

"No, not yet," she said. "That tiger may still be down there, waiting and hiding. You and Jacko and Bumpo, and Choo and Chaa stay up here, and pretty soon I will give you a new lesson."

"Oh, a new lesson!" exclaimed Jacko. "I wonder what kind it will be. We have learned to swing by our tails, and to hang by one paw. Is there anything else we can learn?"

"Many things," said the mamma monkey, for she and her husband had been teaching the children the different things monkeys must know to get along in the woods.

So the four little monkeys sat in the tree in front of their home, and waited for their mother to teach them a new lesson.

If you had seen Mappo's house, you would not have thought it a very nice one. It was just some branches of a tree, twined together, over a sort of platform, or floor, of dried branches. About all the house was used for was to keep off some of the rain that fell very heavily in the country where Mappo lived.

But this house suited the monkeys very well. They did not need to have a warm one, for it was never winter in the land where they lived. It was always hot and warm—sometimes too warm. There was never any snow or ice, but, instead, just rain. It rained half the year, and the other half it was dry. So, you see, Mappo's house was only needed to keep off the rain.

Mappo and the other monkeys did not stay in their houses very much. They went in them to sleep, but that was about all. The rest of the time they jumped about in the trees, looking for things to eat, and, once in a while, when there was no danger, they went down on the ground to play.

"I guess that tiger is gone now," said Jacko to Mappo. "Let's go down on the ground again, and get some of those green things that are good to eat."

The little monkeys had been eating some fruit, like green pears, which they liked very much, when the tiger came along and frightened them. Tigers would rather eat monkeys than green pears, I guess.

"Yes, I think we can go down now," said Mappo, looking through the leaves, and seeing nothing of the savage, striped tiger.

"You'd better ask mamma," said Choo, one of the little girl monkeys.

"Indeed I will not! I can see as good as she can that the tiger isn't there!" exclaimed Mappo.

You see monkey children don't want to mind, and be careful, any more than some human children do.

Mappo started to climb down the tree, holding on to the branches by his four paws and by his tail. He was almost to the ground, and Jacko and

Bumpo were following him, when, all at once, there was a dreadful roar, and out sprang the tiger again.

"Oh, run! Run quick! Jump back!" screamed Mappo, and he and his brothers got back to their tree-house not a second too soon. The tiger snapped his teeth, and growled, he was so mad at being fooled the second time.

"Here! What did I tell you monkeys? You must stay up in the tree!" chattered Mrs. Monkey, as she jumped out of the house. She had been inside shaking up the piles of leaves that were the beds for her family.

"We—we thought the tiger was gone," said Mappo, who was trembling because he was so frightened.

"But he wasn't," said Bumpo, shivering.

"No, he was right there," added Jacko, looking around.

"Yes, and he'll be there for some time," said Mrs. Monkey. "I told you to be careful. Now you just sit down, all of you, and don't you dare stir out of this tree until I tell you to. I'll let you know when the tiger is gone," and she looked down through the leaves toward the ground.

"He is still there," said Mrs. Monkey, for she caught sight of the stripes of the tiger's skin. She had very sharp eyes, and though the patches of sunlight through the jungle leaves hid the bad creature somewhat, Mrs. Monkey could tell he was there, waiting to catch one of her little children.

"Your father will be coming along, soon," said Mrs. Monkey, to her children. "The tiger may lay in wait for him. I'd better let him know he must be careful as he comes along through the woods."

So Mrs. Monkey raised up her head, and called as loudly as she could, in her chattering talk. You would not have understood what she said, even if you had heard it, though there are some men who say they can understand monkey talk.

But the other monkeys in the woods heard what the mother of Mappo was saying, and they, too, began to shout, in their language:

"Look out for the tiger! There is a tiger hiding down under the bushes! Look out for him!"

Soon the whole jungle was filled with the sound of the chattering of the monkeys, as, one after another, they began to shout. It was a warning they shouted—a warning to Mr. Monkey to be careful when he came near his home—to be careful of the tiger lying in wait for him.

My! what a noise those monkeys made, shouting and chattering in the jungle. You could hear them for a mile or more. It was their way of telephoning to Mappo's papa. Monkeys cannot really telephone, you know—that is, not the way we do—but they can shout, one after another, so as to be heard a long way off.

First one would chatter something about the tiger—then another monkey, farther off, would take up the cry, and so on until Mr. Monkey heard it. So it was as good as a telephone, anyhow.

As soon as Mappo's papa, who had gone a long distance from the tree-house to look for some bananas for his family—as soon as he heard the shouting about the tiger, he said to himself:

"Well, I must get home as quickly as I can, to look after my family. But I'll be careful. I hope Mappo and the others will stay in the tall trees."

For Mr. Monkey well knew that if his wife and little ones stayed up in the high trees the tiger could not very well get at them, though tigers can sometimes climb low trees.

Meanwhile Mrs. Monkey was keeping good watch over her little ones. They had no idea, now, of going down on the ground to play—at least as long as the tiger was hiding near them in the bushes.

"But I wish we had something to do," said Mappo, who was a merry little chap, always laughing, shouting, running about or playing some trick on his brothers and sisters. Just then he thought of a little trick.

He went softly up behind Jacko, and tickled him on the ear with a long piece of a tree branch. Jacko thought it was a fly, and put up his paw to brush it away. Mappo pulled the tree branch away just in time, and while Jacko was peeling the skin off a bit of fruit, to eat it, Mappo again tickled his brother.

"Oh that fly!" chattered Jacko. "If I get hold of him!" and again he brushed with his paw at what he thought was a fly.

This made Mappo laugh. The merry little monkey laughed so hard that the next time he tried to tickle Jacko, Mappo's paw slipped, and Jacko, turning around, saw his brother.

"Oh ho! So it was you, and not a fly!" cried Jacko. He dropped his fruit, and raced after his brother. Up through the tree, nearly to the top, went the two monkeys, as fast as they could. They laughed and chattered, for it was all in fun.

Finally Jacko caught Mappo by the tail.

"Oh, let go!" begged Mappo.

"Will you stop tickling me?" asked Jacko.

"I guess so—maybe!" laughed Mappo, trying to pull his tail out of his brother's paw.

"No, you'll have to say for sure, before I let you go!"

Jacko pulled pretty hard on Mappo's tail.

"Oh! let go! Yes, I'll be good! I won't tickle you any more!" cried Mappo.

Then Jacko let go, and started to climb down the tree to the little platform in front of the monkey house. But Mappo was not done with his jokes. He scrambled down faster than did Jacko, and finally, when Jacko was not looking, Mappo grasped the end of his brother's tail, and gave it a hard pinch.

"Ouch! Oh dear! Mamma, the tiger's got me!" cried Jacko.

"Ha! Ha! That's the time I fooled you!" laughed Mappo in his chattering way.

Then Jacko gave chase after Mappo again, and the two monkey boys were having lots of fun in the trees, when Mrs. Monkey called to them:

"Jacko! Mappo! Come down here. It is time for your new lesson. And you, too, Choo and Chaa! You'll have time to practice a little bit before your father comes home," and she looked down to see if the tiger were there.

But the bad animal had gone away. He had heard the monkeys talking about him, and sending a warning all through the jungle where they lived. A jungle, you know, is a great big woods.

"What lesson is it going to be, Mamma?" asked Mappo.

"You'll soon see," she said.

And Mrs. Monkey went into the tree-house, came out with a brown, shaggy thing, about as big as a small football. Have you ever seen one of those? Only, of course, it was not a football.

"Oh, what is it, Mamma?" asked Chaa.

"I know!" exclaimed Bumpo, as he tried to climb under a branch, and bumped his head.

"Ouch!" he cried.

That was why he was called Bumpo—he was always bumping his head, though it did not hurt him very much, for he was covered with a heavy growth of hair.

"Well, what is it, if you know?" asked Mappo, for he was looking at the big, round, brown thing, and trying to guess what it was.

"It's—it's a new kind of banana," said Bumpo, for he and his brothers and sisters were very fond of the soft red and yellow fruit.

"No, it isn't a banana," said Mrs. Monkey. "It's a cocoanut."

"I never saw a cocoanut as big as that," spoke Mappo, for his papa had brought some smaller, round nuts to the tree-house, and had said they were cocoanuts. The little monkeys had not been allowed to eat any of the white meat inside the cocoanut though, for they were too small for it then.

"Yes, this is a cocoanut," went on Mrs. Monkey. "You are now getting large enough to have some for your meals, and so I am going to give you a lesson in how to open a cocoanut."

"I thought cocoanut was white," said Choo.

"It is, inside," said Mrs. Monkey. "This cocoanut I now have has the outer shell still on it. That is why it is not round, like some you may have seen. Inside this soft covering is the round nut, and inside that round nut is the white meat. Now, Mappo, you are a smart little monkey, let me see if you will know how to open the cocoanut. And, when you do, you may all have some to eat."

Mappo took the cocoanut and looked at it. He turned it over and over in his paws. Then, with his fingers, he tried to pull it apart. But he could not do it. The nut was too hard for him. Next he tried to bite it open, but he could not.

"Let me try. I can open it!" exclaimed Jacko.

"No, I'll do it," said Mappo.

"If you can't, I can," spoke Bumpo, and he gave a jump over toward Mappo, and once more he hit his head on a branch, Bumpo did.

"Ouch!" he chattered, rubbing the sore place with his paw.

Mappo turned the cocoanut over and over again. He was looking for some hole in it through which he could put his paw and get out the white meat. But he saw none.

"Maybe I could open it," said Choo, gently.

"No, we must let Mappo have a good try," said Mrs. Monkey. "Then, if he cannot do it, you may all have a turn. But it is a good lesson to know how to open a cocoanut. When you get to be big monkeys, you will have to open a great many of them."

Mappo was pulling and tearing at the hard husk of the cocoanut.

"If I had something sharp, I could tear it open," he said. Then he happened to look up in the tree, and he saw where a branch had been broken off, leaving a sharp point.

"Ha! I have it!" he cried.

He broke off the branch, and with the sharp point he soon had torn a hole in the outer husk of the cocoanut. He pulled the round nut out.

"I have it!" he chattered.

"Yes, but it isn't good to eat yet," said Bumpo. "How are you going to open the rest of it?"

Mappo did not know. Once more he tried to bite a hole, but he could not. All of a sudden the nut slipped from his paws, and fell down toward the ground.

"Oh!" cried Mappo, and he started to climb down after the nut. "My cocoanut is lost!"

"Look out for the tiger!" cried Jacko. "Look out, Mappo!"

CHAPTER II

MAPPO PLAYS A TRICK

Mappo, who had started to climb down to the ground, to get the cocoanut he had lost, stopped short when he heard his brother Jacko cry out about the tiger.

"Don't be afraid," said Mrs. Monkey. "The tiger is not there now. He has gone, or else I shouldn't have let you try to open the cocoanut, Mappo. Go on and get it; don't be afraid."

So Mappo went on down to the ground. And, when he reached it, he saw something that was very strange to him.

"Oh, Mamma!" cried Mappo. "The cocoanut is all broken to pieces. I can pick out the white meat now. Oh, Mamma, it's all broken."

"Is it?" cried Bumpo, and he hurried down so fast that he hit his nose, and sneezed.

"Yes, it's all cracked open," said Mappo. "Oh, goodie!"

Of course Mappo didn't just say that in so many words, but he talked, in his monkey talk, just as you children would have done, had the same thing happened to you.

"Maybe the tiger broke open the cocoanut for you," said Bumpo, as he rubbed his hurt nose.

"No, the tiger is not there," said Mrs. Monkey. "You may all go down and see how Mappo opened the cocoanut."

Down trooped all the five little monkeys, Mappo was the first to reach his cocoanut.

"Why!" he cried. "It fell on a stone, and smashed open. That's what cracked the shell, Mamma."

"Yes, I thought it would," said Mrs. Monkey. "And that is the lesson you little ones are to learn. You cannot bite open a cocoanut. You must crack it on a stone. Mappo dropped his by accident, but it can also be dropped, or thrown, on purpose. So, when you get a cocoanut, the first thing to do is to get a sharp stick, and take off the outer shell. Then, go up in a tall tree, and drop the inside nut down on a stone. The fall will break it, and you can then eat the white meat."

"Oh, isn't that a nice thing to know!" cried Choo.

"Yes, indeed," said her sister Chaa. "I wish we had a cocoanut to break open."

"Come up in the tree and I'll give you each one," said Mrs. Monkey.

Up into the tree, where their house was, scrambled Mappo, and his brothers and sisters. Mappo carried in his paws the pieces of white cocoanut he had broken out of the round, brown shell. He nibbled at a piece.

"Oh, doesn't that taste good!" he cried.

"Please give me some," begged Chaa, holding out one little, brown paw.

"No, I want it all," said Mappo.

"Oh, you must not be selfish!" said Mrs. Monkey. "Give your brothers and sisters some, Mappo, and when they open their nuts, they will give you some."

Mappo was sorry he had been a little selfish. He gave each of the other monkeys some cocoanut. Mrs. Monkey went into the tree-house and came out with four other cocoanuts. She gave one each to the other monkeys, and soon they had torn off the tough, outer husk, or covering, with a sharp stick, the way Mappo did.

Then they threw the round brown nuts down on a flat stone under the tree, cracking the shell so they could pick out the white meat.

"Oh, but this is good!" exclaimed Mappo, as he chewed some of the pieces his brothers and sisters gave him.

All of a sudden, as the little monkeys were eating away, there sounded a rustling in the trees. Something was coming through the branches.

"Look out!" cried Jacko.

"Run!" shouted Mappo.

"Don't be afraid, children, it's only your papa," said a kind, chattering voice, and Mr. Monkey, with a bunch of bananas slung over his back, came scrambling up to the tree-house.

"Did you see the tiger?" asked Mrs. Monkey.

"No, but I heard the other monkeys calling out about him, so I was careful," said the papa monkey. "Are you all right here?"

"Oh, yes. We saw him in time," spoke Mrs. Monkey.

"Oh, papa, I can open a cocoanut!" cried Mappo.

"So can I!" exclaimed Bumpo. "Look!" and he was in such a hurry to show what he could do that he slipped, and bumped his head against Mappo, nearly knocking him off the branch on which the monkey boy was sitting.

In fact, Mappo did fall off, but he had his tail tightly wound around the branch, so he did not fall all the way to the ground, as he might have done.

"Look out! What are you doing?" cried Mappo to Bumpo, after having swung himself up on the branch again.

"Oh dear! I'm sorry. I didn't mean to," said Bumpo. "I just wanted to show papa how I can open a cocoanut."

"We can all open cocoanuts! We've had our lessons," said Chaa.

"Good!" cried Mr. Monkey. "To open cocoanuts is a good thing to know. And now here are some bananas I have brought you." He passed around the yellow fruit from the bunch he had brought home. Then, having eaten bananas and cocoanut, all the monkeys went to sleep.

That is about all monkeys in the jungle do—eat and sleep. Of course some of the younger ones play tricks once in a while. Monkeys are very mischievous and fond of playing tricks. That is what makes them so funny in the circus, and with the hand-organ men.

When the monkeys awakened, they were thirsty. Mappo was going down, right away, to the ground and get a drink at a water-pool near the family tree.

"Wait!" called his father, stretching out his long, hairy arms. "I must first look to see that the tiger is not there, Mappo."

But the tiger was far away, so the monkeys scrambled down and took long drinks. Then they crawled back into their tree again.

For two or three days after this, Mappo, his brothers and sisters practiced their new lesson of opening cocoanuts, until they could do it as well as Mr. and Mrs. Monkey.

Meanwhile they had gone off together, a little way into the woods, looking for different things to eat. Mappo used to go a little ahead of the others.

"Be careful," his mother warned him. "If you get too far away from us, the tiger will catch you."

Then Mappo would come back.

One day, after the monkeys had opened some cocoanuts and eaten out the white meat, Mappo thought of a good trick to play on Bumpo or Jacko.

Down on the ground, under the family tree, were some empty cocoanut shells. One was almost whole, with only a small piece broken out.

"I'll put that piece of shell back in the hole," said Mappo, "and it will look as though it had not been opened. Then I'll give it to Jacko or Bumpo. They'll think it's a good cocoanut, and try to break it open. Then won't they feel funny when they see it's empty!"

Mappo was thinking so much about the trick he was going to play, that he did not look about, as he ought to have done, for any signs of danger. He was down on the ground, putting the piece of shell back in the hole in the empty cocoanut, to play a trick on one of his brothers, when, all of a sudden, there was a crashing in the bushes, right in front of Mappo, and out jumped the big, yellow and black striped tiger.

"Oh my!" exclaimed Mappo, and he was so frightened that he could not move.

CHAPTER III

MAPPO IN A NET

Mappo crouched down on the ground, trying to hide under a green bush of the jungle. In his paw he held the empty cocoanut shell with which he was going to play a trick on Bumpo or Jacko. The tiger was creeping, slowly, slowly along, on his soft, padded feet, just as your cat creeps after a bird. Mappo was too frightened to move.

"Ah ha!" growled the tiger, away down deep in his throat. "At last I have caught a monkey!"

Of course he had not yet really caught Mappo, but he soon would; there was very little doubt of that. Mappo shivered. He wished he had not tried to play the trick. If he had stayed safe up in the tree, the tiger could not have gotten at him.

Mappo, with his queer little eyes, almost like yours, looked up toward where he knew his tree-house was. He was looking to see if his papa or mamma were in sight.

"Ha! There is no use looking up there!" said the cunning tiger, lashing his striped sides with his long tail. "There's no one up there to help you!"

Poor Mappo saw that this was so. There was none of his brothers or sisters up in the tree-house. Nor was his papa or mamma there. The whole monkey family had gone off to look for more cocoanuts, since those they had had were all eaten up.

Just before starting out Mrs. Monkey had said:

"Where is Mappo?"

"Oh, he just went on ahead," said Bumpo, who had seen his brother scrambling down the tree toward the ground. Bumpo did not know what his brother was going to do, or that Mappo intended to play a trick with the empty cocoanut shell.

"Oh, if he's gone on ahead, then we'll catch up to him," said Mrs. Monkey. So away they all went, leaving the tree-house empty, and expecting to meet Mappo somewhere on the road through the jungle.

But they did not, and there was poor Mappo on the ground right in front of the bad tiger. The tiger knew none of the monkey family was near the tree-house except Mappo. That was what made the tiger so bold.

For, had Mr. Monkey, or Mrs. Monkey, been at home they would have seen, or smelled the tiger. Monkeys, and other creatures of the jungle, can often smell danger much better and more quickly than they can see it. And, had Mr. or Mrs. Monkey smelled the tiger, they would have kept their little ones safe in the tree, and would have shouted loudly, to warn all the other monkeys of the danger of the bad tiger.

"Well, you can't get away from me this time!" growled the tiger, speaking in his own language, which Mappo understood very well, just as the tiger understood the monkey talk.

For, though monkeys, tigers and elephants, as well as cats and dogs, cannot speak our language, they have a way of their own for talking one to another. To us it may sound only like chatter, growls, meows and barks, but it is really talk. Wouldn't it be nice if we could understand animals as well as they understand us?

For they can understand our talk, you know. Else how would a horse know when to start and stop, when the driver tells him? Or how would your dog know when to come to you, and to lie down when you tell him to, if he didn't understand you? Tell me that, if you please.

So Mappo understood the tiger, and the tiger understood Mappo.

The little monkey, still keeping tight hold of the empty cocoanut shell, looked at the crouching tiger as bravely as he could. Nearer and nearer crept the striped beast. But don't you be afraid. I have a way of saving Mappo, and I'm going to do it, too!

"Chatter! Chatter! Chip! Chip! Whew! Zur-r-r-r-r!" went Mappo in his queer monkey talk. That was his way of calling for help. All monkeys do that in the jungle, when they are in danger. They want a whole lot more monkeys to come and help them.

"There's no use in your calling that way!" growled the tiger, deep in his throat. "Nobody can hear you!"

Mappo began to believe that this was so. All the monkeys seemed to have gone away from that part of the jungle. He was all alone with the tiger.

Now Mappo was a brave little chap, but being brave is not going to do one much good, when there's a tiger in the way. So Mappo thought, besides being brave, he might be polite, and ask a favor of the tiger. For animals are often more kind to one another than we think. If you watch them sometimes, as I have done, you will see that this is so.

So Mappo made up his mind he would ask the tiger, as a favor, not to bite or eat him.

"And, if he won't be kind to me," thought Mappo, "well, then maybe something else will happen. Maybe papa will come, with a whole lot more monkeys, and drive the tiger away. Or, if he does not, well, maybe something else will happen," and Mappo looked at the empty cocoanut shell in his paw.

"Please let me go, Mr. Tiger!" begged Mappo. "I never did anything to you. Let me go!"

"No. I'll not!" growled the tiger. "I'm hungry and I want something to eat. I chased after a goat half the morning, but it got away from me. Then I tried to get a little deer, but it ran back with the rest of the deer, and, as the big deer had such sharp horns, I dared not go after it. So I haven't had anything to eat, and I'm very hungry. You haven't any horns, none of your monkey friends are near, and I'm going to eat you!"

Mappo looked to see how far it was to the nearest tree. It was some distance off, but the little monkey boy knew if he could reach it he would be safe. For, in the tree, he could run much faster, from branch to branch, than could the tiger on the ground. But in getting over the ground on his four paws the monkey was a bit slow. And the tiger, in one jump could grab Mappo if the monkey started to run.

"Well, there's no use trying to get away from him by running on the ground," thought Mappo. "He'd have me in a second. And there's no use asking a favor of him. He seems to be mad at me. I wonder how I can get away from him!"

Once more Mappo looked at the empty cocoanut shell in his paw—the shell with which he was going to play a trick on Jacko or Bumpo.

Nearer and nearer to Mappo crept the tiger, lashing his tail from side to side. Tigers always do that, just as cats do when they are trying to catch a bird in the garden. Tigers are only big cats, you know, very much bigger and stronger than your pussy. And they always creep slowly, slowly up toward anything they are going to catch, until they are near enough to give one jump and grab it in their claws. That is what the tiger was trying to do to Mappo.

All of a sudden Mappo raised the paw that held the cocoanut shell. The little monkey chap made up his mind to be brave and save himself if he could.

"Take that, Mr. Tiger!" called Mappo, all at once.

With all his might he threw the empty cocoanut shell right at the tiger's head. Monkeys are very good throwers. They are almost as good as are baseball boys at that sort of thing.

"Bang!" went the cocoanut on the tiger's head. It cracked open—I mean the cocoanut cracked open—where Mappo had stuck it together. It made quite a noise.

"Oh my!" cried the tiger, jumping up suddenly, for he did not know what to make of the cocoanut shell in his face. Mappo had thrown it so suddenly.

Then, as the tiger heard the cracking of the cocoanut shell, he thought it was his own head. Tigers are sometimes silly that way, no matter if they are strong, and have sharp claws.

"Oh my head! My head!" cried the tiger. "It is broken!"

You see he really thought it was. The crack of the cocoanut shell made him think that it was his own silly, bad head.

Up in the air reared the tiger on his hind legs. This was just the chance Mappo wanted.

"Here I go!" thought the little monkey chap. "Here's where I get away."

As fast as Mappo could go he scrambled over the ground toward the tree where his house was built. By this time the tiger had seen the empty cocoanut shell fall to the ground, and the striped creature knew what had happened.

"Ha! That monkey boy! He did that!" growled the tiger. "He can't fool me that way! I'll get him! I'll fix him for playing tricks on me!"

Finding that his head was all right, and not cracked as he had feared it was, the tiger gave a big jump, and ran after Mappo. But Mappo was not waiting for him. The little monkey boy was now far across the open place on the ground, and was climbing up into a tree as fast as he could go.

"Come back here!" growled the tiger, making a spring for Mappo. But Mappo was safely out of the way. The tiger's claws stuck in the trunk of the tree, tearing loose some bits of bark, but Mappo was not hurt. He got safely away.

Then, sitting up in the tree on a high limb, Mappo, as he looked down at the tiger, chattered:

"Ha! You didn't get me after all! You didn't catch me! I fooled you! Chatter-chatter-chat! Bur-r-r-r! Wuzzzzzzz! Whir-r-r-r-r!"

That's the way Mappo chattered, not so much to make fun of the bad tiger, as to warn the other monkeys in the woods that the bad striped animal was near, and that there was danger in the jungle.

"Chatter-chatter-chat! Bur-r-r-r-r! Whe-e-e-e-e! Zir-r-r-r!" chattered the other monkeys, far off in the jungle, as they heard Mappo's warning. The woods were filled with the sound they made.

"Well, I might as well go away," thought the tiger. "They will all be on the lookout for me now. I'll have to wait until after dark to catch a monkey, or something else to eat. Bur-r-r-r-r! But I'm hungry!"

So the tiger slunk away, and I guess no one else in the woods felt sorry that he had not caught Mappo. They were all glad the monkey boy had gotten away, and Mappo was especially glad, on his own account.

"Ha! That was a good trick of yours—to throw the empty cocoanut shell at the tiger, Mappo," said an old grandfather monkey, high in a tree. Mappo had told his friends, the other monkeys, what had happened.

"Yes, indeed it was," said an uncle monkey. "Mappo is a smart boy to think of such a trick."

This made Mappo feel pretty proud of himself.

"Do you know where my papa and mamma are?" he asked.

"They went off over toward the banana grove," said the grandfather monkey. "Be careful of the tiger if you follow them."

"I will," promised Mappo. But the tiger had slunk away now, so Mappo thought it would be safe to travel through the jungle, especially if he kept up in the trees, and did not go down on the ground.

Off Mappo started after his folks, who had gone on, thinking to catch up to him.

Mappo had not gone very far before he came to a place in the woods where he saw something very strange. It was strange and also nice, for, down on the ground, were a number of pieces of white cocoanut.

"Well, that's good!" thought Mappo. "Cocoanut already shelled to eat. I wonder who could have left that there for me. Maybe my papa or mamma did, knowing I would come this way. Yes, that must be it. They are very kind to me. I'll go down and get some of that sweet cocoanut."

Now Mappo was not a very wise little monkey. He had not lived long enough to know all the dangers of the jungle. There were dangers from tigers and other wild beasts.

Some of those dangers Mappo knew about, and he also knew how to keep out of their way. But there were other dangers from men—from hunters—and these Mappo did not know so well. For, as yet, he had never seen a man—a human being. Mappo had only lived in the jungle where men very seldom came, and those men were brown or black men.

But men knew monkeys were in the woods, and men wanted the monkeys for circuses, for menageries and for hand-organs. That is the reason men try to catch monkeys.

Mappo looked all around the forest from the top of the tree where he had come to rest. He saw no signs of danger. He saw only white pieces of cocoanut on the ground.

"I'll go down and get some, and then I'll run on and find my papa and mamma and brothers and sisters," thought Mappo. "They will want some of this cocoanut."

Down he went, and began picking up the bits of cocoanut. They were rather small pieces and Mappo had to eat a great many of them before he felt he had enough. Each piece was a little way beyond the next one, and Mappo kept on walking along slowly as he picked them up.

Finally he saw a very large piece. He reached for it with his paw, and then, all at once something happened.

Something like a big spider's web seemed to fall down out of a tree right over Mappo. In an instant he was all tangled up—his paws and tail were caught. He yelled and chattered in fright, and tried to get loose, but the more he tried, the tighter the meshes of the net fell about him.

Poor Mappo was caught. He had been caught by a hunter's net in the jungle, and the pieces of cocoanut were only bait, just as you bait a mouse trap with cheese.

"Oh!" cried Mappo, in his shrill, chattering voice. "Oh dear! I am caught!"

Tighter and tighter the net closed over him.

CHAPTER IV

MAPPO IN A BOX

Poor Mappo was not a merry monkey just then. Usually he was a jolly little fellow, laughing and chattering in his own way, and playing tricks on his brothers and sisters. Now he felt very little like doing anything of that sort.

"And to think that I was going to play a trick with the empty cocoanut shell, just a little while before this happened to me," thought Mappo, as he tried very hard to get loose from the net in which he was all tangled up. "I wonder what has happened to me, anyhow," said Mappo to himself.

And, as Mappo did not find out for some little time I will tell you. He had been caught by a native hunter, in a net made from long pieces of a trailing vine, which was as strong as a rope.

In the country where Mappo lived there were many people called natives—that is they had never lived in any country but their own, and they were a queer sort of people.

They wore very few clothes, for it was too hot to need many. They were a black, savage people, and they lived by hunting with their spears, and bows and arrows. They hunted wild animals—lions, tigers, elephants and monkeys. Some of the wild animals they used for food, and others they sold to white men who wanted them for circuses and menageries. And monkeys were generally the easiest to catch.

Some of these black, half-clothed, savage natives had spread a vine net in the forest. The net, being made of vines, could not be seen until some animal got close to it. And to make monkeys come close to the net, so it would fall down over them, when one end was pulled loose by a native (hidden behind a tree) bits of cocoanut were sprinkled about. Monkeys are very fond of cocoanut, and the natives knew, when the little long-tailed creatures went to pick up the white pieces, that they would come nearer and nearer to the trap-net, until they were caught. That was what had happened to Mappo.

The little monkey tried and tried again to break out of the net, but he could not. It was too strong. Tighter and tighter it was pulled about him, until he could struggle no more. He lay there, a sad little lump of monkey in the net.

Then some black men, with long sharp sticks, or spears, gathered about him, and talked very fast and loud. You would not have understood what they said, if you had heard them, any more than you can understand dog and cat talk, but Mappo knew some of what they were saying, for he had lived in the jungle all his life, and these were natives, or jungle men.

"Ha! We caught only one monkey!" exclaimed one tall, black man, with a long spear.

"Well, but he is a good one," another man said. "We will take him to the coast in a box, and sell him to the white men who will take him away in a ship. We will get many things for him, lots of beads to put around our necks, some brass wire to make rings for our noses and ankles, and red cloth to wear."

The natives, you see, did not want money. They wanted beads and bits of shiny brass wire, or gay-colored cloth, to make themselves look, as they thought, very fine. They even put rings in their noses, as well as in their ears, to decorate themselves.

"Ha! So this is not the end of me!" thought Mappo, when he heard the black men thus talking. "I am to be put in a box, and taken to a ship, it seems. I wonder what a ship is like. Well, as long as I am not to be hurt, perhaps it will be fun after all. But I wish they would let my mamma and papa, and sisters and brothers come with me. It is no fun being all by yourself."

But of course Mappo's folks were, by this time, a long way off in the jungle woods, wondering where Mappo himself was. If they had seen him in the net, they might have tried to get him out, but they did not see him.

The net was now pulled so tightly about the little monkey, that he was in some pain.

"Bring up the box, and we'll put him in it," said one of the black men.

Another native came up with a box made of tree branches nailed together. It was what is called a crate—that is, there were spaces between the slats so Mappo could look out and get air.

"Look out. He may bite you!" called one native to another, as the crate was placed near the net.

"Oh, I won't give him a chance!" the other native said.

"Ha! I won't bite!" chattered Mappo, but the natives did not understand him. They knew very little of monkey talk. Mappo made up his mind that he would be good, for his mamma had often told him that was the best way to get along in this world. "But I'm sure she never thought I would be caught in a net," said Mappo to himself. "I wonder if she would mean me to be good now; and not bite. I guess she would, so I won't nip anybody."

Mappo had very sharp teeth, even if he was a monkey, and he could give some good hard bites. But now he was going to be good.

The net, with poor Mappo in it, was dragged up close to the crate, and a door in the crate was opened. Then part of the net was pulled to one side, and Mappo saw a hole where he thought he might slip out. He gave a jump, hoping he could get back into the tall trees again.

"And if I do, I'll never eat any more cocoanut, unless my mamma or papa gives it to me!" thought Mappo.

So he gave a jump out of the net, but, in a second he found himself inside the wooden crate, or box. He had gone into it when the net was open opposite the door of the crate. In another second the door was shut and fastened, and Mappo was a prisoner in a new prison. He could not get out, no matter how hard he tried.

"There he is, safe and sound!" chattered the natives, in their queer language, which was as much like monkey talk as anything else. "Now we can carry him to the coast, and sell him to the white men. Come on."

"I wonder where the coast is," thought Mappo, and I might tell you, in case you don't know, that the coast is the seashore.

The ships, in which white men come to the jungle countries, go only as far as the seashore. They cannot go on the land, or into the interior, where the wild animals live. So when the natives catch monkeys, or other creatures, they have to carry them to the coast.

"Well, this isn't very nice," thought Mappo, as he looked at the little crate, inside of which he now found himself. "I haven't much room to move around here, and I don't see anything to eat, or drink."

He was not very hungry, for he had eaten a lot of the cocoanut just before being caught in the net. But he was thirsty. However, he saw no water, and, though he chattered, and asked for it as nicely as he knew how, he got none—at least, not right away.

Mappo's fur was all ruffled by being caught in the net, and he now began to smooth that out, until he looked more like himself. He peered through between the slats of his cage with his queer little eyes, and there was a sad look in them, if any one had noticed. But no one did. The natives were getting ready to carry Mappo to the coast.

Poor Mappo looked out on the green jungle where he had lived ever since he could remember. He did not know that he was never to see it again. He would never climb the big trees, and swing from one branch to another. He would not play tag with his brothers and sisters, nor would he open cocoanuts on a sharp stick and by dropping them on a stone. Mappo was to be taken away from his nice jungle.

Of course he did not know all this at once. All he knew now was that he was in a little crate, where he had hardly room enough to turn around, and no room at all to hang by his tail.

"Come on—let's start with him!" called one of the black men. "We'll take him to the white people, and come back and catch some more monkeys."

"Oh, I hope they catch some of my folks!" thought Mappo. He did not wish any harm to happen to his father or mother, or sisters or brothers, you know, but he was so lonesome, that he wanted to see some of them.

The natives thrust long poles through the slats of Mappo's box, and, putting the poles over their shoulders, off through the jungle they started to march. Poor Mappo was very thirsty by this time, but though he chattered very hard, and cried "Water!" over and over again, in his monkey language, no one paid any attention to him.

On and on went the natives, carrying the little monkey in a crate. After a while some other black men came along another path, and they, too, had boxes slung on poles, and in the boxes were other animals. In one was a big striped tiger, and when Mappo saw him, the monkey crouched down in a corner of his box and covered his eyes with his paws.

"Oh, maybe it's the same tiger that tried to catch me, and whom I hit on the head with the empty cocoanut," thought Mappo. "If it is, he'll be very angry at me, and try to get me.

"Oh dear! This is too bad. I guess this is the end of me!" Mappo cried.

The natives carrying Mappo, in his box, ran forward with him, and as he looked out, he saw that his crate was close to the one in which was the growling, striped tiger.

"Oh! Oh! Oh!" thought poor Mappo. "He'll get me sure!"

CHAPTER V

MAPPO ON THE SHIP

Mappo, who had taken his paws down from his eyes long enough to look at the striped tiger, now blind-folded himself, with his paws again, and shivered. All of a sudden the tiger growled, and Mappo shivered still more.

"Ha! Growl and roar as much as you like!" called one of the black natives. "You can't get out of there, Sharp-Tooth!" That was the name the jungle men had given the tiger. "You can't get out of that crate!" went on the native, and when Mappo heard that, he took down his paws once more, and looked at the tiger. He was sure it was the same one at whom he had thrown the cocoanut, and he wondered how the fierce, strong beast had been caught. Then Mappo looked at the crate in which the tiger was being carried along through the jungle.

"Ha! That is a good, strong crate!" thought Mappo. "It is much stronger than the one I am in. I guess the tiger can't get out, and I am glad of it. I mean I am sorry he is shut up, and I am sorry for myself, that I am shut up, and being taken away, but I would not like the tiger to get loose, while I am near him."

And indeed the cage holding the tiger was very strong. It had big pieces of tree branches for slats, and it took eight men to carry it, for the tiger was very heavy. Side by side, slung in their crates on the poles, over the shoulders of the black natives, Mappo and Sharp-Tooth, the tiger, were carried through the jungle.

The tiger kept walking back and forth in his cage. It was just long enough to allow him to take two steps one way, and two steps the other way. And he kept going back and forth all the while, up and down, his red tongue hanging out of his mouth, for it was very hot. His fur, too, was scratched and cut, as though he had fought very hard, before he had let the natives catch him and put him into the crate.

Mappo was not so much afraid now, and once, when his cage was close to that of the tiger, the big, striped beast spoke to the little monkey. Of course he talked in tiger language, which the natives could not understand, but Mappo could.

"Ha! So they caught you too, little monkey?" asked the tiger.

"Yes, I got caught in a net, while I was eating some cocoanut," answered Mappo.

"The cocoanut was bait," said the tiger. "I got caught eating a little goat. The goat was bait, too, and they caught me in a noose that almost choked me. Then they slipped me in this box when I was half dead. If I had had my strength, they never would have gotten me in it!" and the tiger roared and growled, and tried to break out of his crate. But it was too strong—he could not.

"Keep quiet there, Sharp-Tooth!" cried one of the black natives who was marching along beside the tiger's cage. "Keep quiet, or I shall hit you on the nose with a stick," and the black man held up a hard stick. The tiger growled, away down deep in his throat, and kept quiet. But still he spoke to Mappo, now and then.

"Seems to me I have seen you before, somewhere, little monkey," said Sharp-Tooth.

"Yes, you—you tried to eat me, if you please," said Mappo, who spoke politely, because he was still afraid of the tiger.

"Did I?" asked the tiger. "Well, I have to live, you know. And I have eaten so many monkeys that one, more or less, doesn't matter. So I tried to eat you, eh? I wonder why I didn't finish. I usually eat what I set out to."

"I—I hit you on the head with an empty cocoanut shell and ran away," said Mappo.

"Oh, that's so. You did!" exclaimed the tiger. "I thought I remembered you. So you're the chap who played that trick on me, eh? Well, I thought I knew you. Ha! Yes. An empty cocoanut shell! I remember I was quite frightened. I thought my head was broken. But never mind. I forgive you. One shouldn't remember things like that when friends are in trouble. Listen, little monkey, will you do me a favor?"

"What is it?" asked Mappo, wondering how he, a little monkey, could do anything to help a big, strong tiger.

"Will you help me out of this cage?" asked the tiger.

"How can I?" inquired Mappo.

"Very easily," the tiger said. "I know what is going to become of us. We are to be taken to the big ocean-water, and put in a house that floats on the waves." That was what the tiger called a ship; a house that floats on the waves.

"How do you know this is to happen to us?" asked Mappo.

"Because I heard the black men talking of it," said Sharp-Tooth. "And, after a long while, we will land in another country, where there is no jungle, such as we love."

"That will be too bad," Mappo said. "But still, it may be nice in that other country, and we may have many adventures."

"Bah! I do not want adventures!" the tiger growled. "All I want is to be left alone in my jungle, where I can kill what I want to eat, drink from the jungle pool, and sleep in the sun. I hate these men! I hate this cage! Oncc before I was caught and put in one, but I broke out and got away. This time they have been too strong for me. But you can help me to escape."

"How?" asked Mappo.

"Listen!" whispered the tiger, putting his big mouth, filled with sharp teeth, close to the side of his cage, and nearest to Mappo's crate. "Listen! Your paws are like hands and fingers. To-night, when the natives set our crates down, to take their sleep, you can open your cage, slip out and come over and open mine. I have tried to open my own, but I cannot. However, you can easily do it. Then we will both be free, and we can run away to the jungle together: Come, will you do it? I am very hungry! I want to get off in the jungle and get something to eat."

Mappo thought for a minute. He was a smart little monkey, and he feared if he opened the tiger's cage for him, the big chap might be so hungry that he would eat the first thing he saw, which would be Mappo himself.

"Will you open my cage for me after dark?" asked Sharp-Tooth.

"I'll think about it," answered back Mappo.

But he had no idea of letting out that tiger.

"I'm sure he must still be angry at me for hitting him with that empty cocoanut," said Mappo, "and if he is loose he can easily crush me with one stroke of his paw. No, I think I will not let him out, though I am sorry he is caught. But I will try to get out myself, and run back to my mamma and papa, and sisters and brothers. Yes, I will do that."

After the tiger had asked Mappo to help him get out of the cage, Sharp-Tooth pretended to go to sleep. He wanted to fool the natives, you see, and make believe he was going to be good and gentle.

"Oh, but won't I roar and bite and scratch when I do get out!" thought the tiger. Perhaps he would not have hurt Mappo, had the monkey opened the cage; but I cannot be sure of that.

All day long through the jungle tramped the natives, carrying the wild animals in their crates. There were several besides Mappo and Sharp-Tooth. There were snakes, in big boxes, other monkeys, a rhinoceros, a hippopotamus, two lions, who roared dreadfully all the while, and many other beasts.

In fact, it was a small circus marching through the jungle, and all the animals had been caught, in one way or another, to be sold to circuses and menageries. But in this book I will tell you mostly about Mappo, just as in other books I have told you of Squinty, the comical pig, and Slicko, the jumping squirrel.

"Oh, I do wish I had something to eat!" thought poor Mappo. But he did not see anything for a long time. It was getting dark when the natives, carrying the crates, set them down in the jungle, and began to build fires to cook their supper. They were going to camp out in the woods all night, and they had stopped near a pool of water.

Mappo smelled the water. So did the other animals, and they began to howl for drinks. You remember I told you wild animals can often smell better than they can see.

The natives did not want to be cruel to the animals; they only wanted to sell them to the white people. And the natives knew if the animals did not get something to drink, they might die. So, pretty soon, they began to give the beasts water to drink. Mappo got some, and oh! how good it was to his little dry throat and mouth.

"Don't forget, you are going to let me loose in the night," whispered the tiger to Mappo, as it grew darker and darker in the jungle. Mappo said nothing. He pretended to be asleep. But, all the same, he made up his mind that he was not going to let the tiger loose.

When it was all dark and quiet in the camp, Mappo tried to open his own cage with his smart little fingers. But the natives were smarter than the little monkey. They knew all monkeys were very good at picking open boxes, so they had made this one, for Mappo, especially tight. Mappo tried his best, but he could not get out.

So, after all, he did not have to play any trick on the tiger, and not let Sharp-Tooth out, and he was glad of it.

"Hist! Hist!" the tiger called, from his crate, near that of Mappo. "Aren't you going to let me out?"

"I can't get out myself," answered the little monkey.

"Bur-r-r-r-r! Wow! Wuff!" roared the tiger. And then he was so angry that he growled and jumped about, trying to break out of his cage. The natives awoke, and one of them, running over to Sharp-Tooth, said:

"Quiet here, tiger, or I shall have to hit you on the nose with a stick!"

But the tiger would not be quiet, and, surely enough, the black man hit him on the nose with a stick. The tiger howled and then became quiet. All the other animals who had made different noises when they heard the racket made by Sharp-Tooth, grew quiet also.

Mappo went back to sleep, after trying once more to open his crate so he could get away in the jungle.

"I guess I shall have to let them put me on the house in the big water," he said to himself. "Never mind, I may have some fine adventures."

When morning came, the natives got their breakfast, fed the animals in the crates, and off they started once more through the forest. Mappo looked out of his cage, and he could see, swinging along in the trees on either side of the jungle path, other monkeys like himself. But they were free, and could climb to the tops of the tallest trees.

Mappo called to them, in his own language, and told them to take the news to his papa and mamma that he had been caught in a net, and was being taken away to a far country. The wild monkeys promised that they would let Mr. and Mrs. Monkey know what had become of Mappo.

In this way Mappo's folks learned what had happened to him, but they never saw him again, nor did he see them. But monkeys are not like a boy or girl.

Once they leave their homes, they do not mind it very much. They are always willing to look at something new. Though, of course, they may often wish they were out of their cages, and back in the jungle again.

After some days the natives, with the wild animals, reached the big ocean. Mappo had never seen so much water before. He looked at it through the slats of his crate. A little way out from shore he saw what looked like a big house floating on the water. This was the ship.

Soon, in small boats, all the animals were taken aboard the ship, Mappo among them.

"Now my adventures are really beginning," thought Mappo, as he found himself in a cage on deck, next to some other monkeys, and a big cow with a hump on her back. She was a sacred cow.

CHAPTER VI

MAPPO MEETS TUM TUM

Mappo did not know what a ship was, nor how it floated over the ocean from one country to another, blown by the wind or pushed by steam engines. The little monkey could not see much except the other monkeys in crates on the deck near him. Finally Mappo did hear a deep growl from somewhere behind him.

"Ha!" snarled a voice. "There will be little chance to get away now! Why didn't you let me out of my cage, monkey?"

"I—I couldn't," said Mappo, and he looked around to see the tiger close to him. Sharp Tooth was in his own cage and could not reach Mappo. For this the monkey was very glad.

All the black men who had carried the wild animals through the jungle had gone now. In their places were white men, quite different. Mappo did not know which he liked better, but the white men seemed to be kind, for some of them brought food and water to the animals.

"Are we on the ship, or water-house, now?" asked Mappo, as he felt as though he were being moved along.

"Yes, we are on a ship, and we'll never see the jungle any more," said the tiger. "Oh wow!" and he roared very loudly.

"Quiet there!" called one of the white men, and he banged with his stick on the tiger's cage. The tiger growled, and lay down.

Now it was quiet aboard the ship, which soon started away from the shores of the hot, jungle country toward another land, where it is warm part of the time and cold part of the time. Mappo was on his way to have many new adventures.

For several days the little monkey boy did nothing but stay in his cage, crouched in one corner, looking out between the slats. He could see nothing, for, all around him, were other cages. But when he looked up, through the top of his cage, he could see a little bit of blue sky.

It was the same kind of blue sky he had looked at from his tree-house in the jungle, now so far away, and Mappo did not feel so lonesome, or homesick, when he watched the white clouds sail over the little patch of blue sky.

For you know animals do get homesick just as do boys and girls. Often, in circuses and menageries, the animals become so homesick, and long so for the land from which they have been taken, that they become ill and die. When a keeper sees one of his pet animals getting homesick, he tries to cure him.

He may put the homesick animal into another cage, or give him different things to eat—things he had in his own country. Or the keeper may put the homesick animal in with some different and new beasts, so the homesick one may have something new to think about. Monkeys very often become homesick, but so do elephants, tigers and lions. It is a sad thing to be homesick, even for animals.

But Mappo was not very homesick. In the first place he was not a very old monkey, and he had not lived in the jungle very long, though he had been there all his life. Then, too, he was anxious to have some adventures.

So, though when he looked at the bit of blue sky, and thought of his home in the deep, green woods, he had a wish, only for a moment, to go back there. He had enough to eat on the ship, plenty of cool water to drink, and he knew he was in no danger from the tiger or other wild beasts bigger than himself. For the tiger was fastened up in a big strong cage, and could not get out.

Mappo, on board the ship, chattered and talked with the other monkeys in cages all around him. He asked how they had been caught, and they told him it was in the same way as he had been—by picking up good things to eat on the ground, and so being tangled up in a net.

"And I don't know what is going to happen to me now," said a little girl monkey, with a very sad face.

"Oh, cheer up!" cried Mappo, in his most jolly voice. "I am sure something nice will happen to all of us. See, we are having a nice ride in the water-house, and we have all we want to eat, without having to hunt for it in the woods."

"Yes, but I want my papa and mamma!" cried the little girl monkey.

Mappo tried to make her feel happier, but it was hard work. As for Mappo, himself, he was feeling pretty jolly, but then he was always a merry monkey.

As the ship sailed on, over the ocean, it left behind the warm, jungle country where Mappo had always lived. The weather grew more cool, and though

Polar Bears like cold weather, and are happy when they have a cake of ice to sit on, monkeys do not. Monkeys must be kept very warm, or they catch cold, just as boys and girls do.

So, as the ship sailed farther and farther north, on its way to a new country, Mappo felt the change. Though he was covered with thick hair, or fur, he could not help shivering, especially at night when the sun had gone down.

The man in charge of the wild animals that were to go to the circus knew how to look after them. He knew which ones had to be kept warm, and which ones cold.

"You must cover up the monkeys' cages these nights," said the man to a sailor one afternoon, as he saw Mappo and the others shivering. "Keep them warm."

"Aye, aye, sir," answered the sailor, which was his way of saying, "Yes, sir!"

Heavy coverings were spread over the monkeys' cages every night, but even then Mappo shivered, and so did the others. It was quite different from the warm jungle where he could sleep out of doors with only his own fur for a bedquilt.

"I guess we'll have to move the monkeys down below, if it gets much colder," said the animal man to the sailor. "They'll freeze up here."

"Free-e-e-e-eze! I-I-I-I—I g-g-g-g-guess we will!" chattered Mappo, and he shivered so that he stuttered when he talked. Of course he spoke monkey language, and the men could not understand him. But they could understand his shivering, and soon they began to move the cages to a warmer place.

Mappo and the other animals who need to be kept warm were lowered through a hole down inside the ship. It was in a place called a "hold." And it was called that, I suppose, because it was made to hold the cargo of wild animals carried by the ship.

Mappo did not like it so well down in this part of the ship as he had liked it on deck. But it was warmer, and that was a great deal. Still he could not see the little patch of blue sky that had reminded him of his jungle home.

"I wonder what has become of Sharp-Tooth, the big tiger?" asked Mappo, of one of the other monkeys.

"Oh, I saw them lower his cage down into another part of the ship," said a big monkey. "I am glad of it, too, for I don't like him so near us. He might break out some night, and bite us."

"He wanted me to let him out," said Mappo.

"Gracious! I hope you didn't think of such a thing!" cried a little girl monkey.

"No, I didn't," Mappo said.

"How did you happen to know the tiger?" asked the big monkey.

"Oh, he tried to get me once," Mappo answered, "and I threw an empty cocoanut shell in his face!"

"You did!" cried all the other monkeys.

"How brave you were!" said the little girl monkey.

Mappo was beginning to feel that way himself!

For several days nothing much happened to Mappo, after he and his monkey friends had been moved to the warm part of the ship. They had things to eat, and water to drink, and they slept a good deal of the time. One day the sailor who always fed Mappo stood in front of the cage, and, looking in, said:

"I wonder if you'd bite me if I petted you a bit? You look like a nice chap, and I like monkeys. I wonder if I couldn't teach you some tricks. Then you'd be worth more to the circus. You'll have to learn tricks in the circus, anyhow, and you might as well begin now. I think I'll pet you a bit."

"Chatter! Chatter! Chat! Bur-r-r-r! Snip!" went Mappo. That meant, in his language, that he would not think of biting the kind sailor who had fed and watered him. But the sailor was careful. Very slowly he put out his hand, and, reaching through the bars, he stroked Mappo's soft fur.

"That's a good chap!" said the sailor. "I believe you are going to be nice after all."

"Bur-r-r-r! Wopp!" said Mappo. That meant: "Of course I am!"

In a few days the sailor and Mappo were good friends, and one afternoon the sailor opened the cage door and let the monkey out. Then Mappo grew quite excited. It was the first time he had been loose since he had been caught, and he was so glad to run about, and use his legs and tail, that, before he knew what he was doing, he had jumped right over the sailor's head, and had scrambled up on the ship's deck.

"Oh, a monkey's loose! One of the monkeys has gotten away!" cried the sailors.

"Never mind! I'll catch him!" said the one who had been kind to Mappo.

Mappo ran and leaped. He saw something like a tall tree, only it had no branches on it. But there were ropes and ladders fast to it, and, in an instant, Mappo had scrambled up them to the top of the tall thing. It was the mast of the ship, but Mappo did not know that.

Away up to the top he went, and, curling his tail around a rope, there he sat.

"Make him come down!" cried the captain. "I can't have a monkey on top of my ship's mast! Somebody climb up after him and bring him down."

"I'll go," said a sailor.

Now a sailor is a good climber, but not nearly so good as a monkey. Mappo waited until the sailor was almost up to him, and then, quick as a flash, Mappo swung himself out of the way by another rope, and, just as he had done in the jungle, he went over to the top of another mast.

"There he goes!" cried the sailors on deck.

"Yes, I see he does," said the sailor who had tried to catch Mappo.

"You had better come down," spoke the man who had let Mappo out of the cage. "I think he'll come down for me." In his hand he held some lumps of sugar, of which Mappo was very fond.

"Come on down, old chap," called the sailor. "No one will hurt you. Come and get the sugar."

Now whether Mappo had had enough of being loose, or whether it was too cold for him up on the mast, I can't say. Perhaps he wanted the sugar, and, again, he might not have wanted to make trouble for his kind friend, the sailor, who had let him out.

Anyhow, Mappo came slowly down, and took some of the sugar from the sailor's hand. The sailor took hold of the collar around Mappo's neck.

"Now lock up that monkey!" cried the captain. "And if he runs away again, we'll whip him."

"No, it was my fault," the sailor said. "And I'd like him to be loose. I can teach him some tricks."

"All right, do as you like," the captain spoke. "Only keep him off the mast."

"I'm not going up there again," thought Mappo to himself. "It is too cold."

"Come along," said the sailor, giving him another lump of sugar, and Mappo put one hairy little paw in the hand of the sailor, and walked along the deck with him.

"I guess you were just scared, old fellow," the man said to the monkey. "When you get quieted down, you and I shall have lots of fun. You are almost as nice as my elephant, Tum Tum."

This was the first Mappo had heard of the elephant. He knew what they were, for he had often seen the big creatures in the jungle, crashing their way through the trees, even pulling some up by the roots, in their strong trunks, to eat the tender green tops of the trees.

"I didn't know there was an elephant on this ship," thought Mappo. But he was soon to find out there was.

Two or three days after this Mappo was let out of his cage once more. This time he did not jump and run. He stayed quietly beside the sailor, and put his paw into the man's hand.

"That's the way to do it," said the sailor. "Come now, we'll go below and see Tum Tum."

Down into a deep part of the ship, near the bottom, the sailor took Mappo. Then the monkey could see a number of elephants chained to the walls. They were swaying their big bodies to and fro, and swinging their trunks. The sailor went up to the biggest elephant of them all, and, so Mappo thought, the most jolly-looking, and said:

"Tum Tum, I have brought some one to see you. Here is a little monkey."

Mappo looked up, and saw a jolly twinkle in the little eyes of Tum Tum. Mappo knew elephants were never unkind to monkeys, and, a moment later, Mappo had given a jump, up to the shoulder of the sailor, and then right on the back of Tum Tum.

CHAPTER VII

MAPPO IN THE CIRCUS

"Well, I declare!" exclaimed the sailor who had brought Mappo downstairs in the ship to see Tum Tum, the jolly elephant. "You two animals seem to get along fine together!"

And indeed Mappo and Tum Tum were the best of friends at once. Elephants and monkeys very seldom quarrel, and they live together in peace, even in the jungle, and do not fight, and bite and scratch, as some wild beasts do.

"Hello!" said Mappo to Tum Tum, as the little monkey sat on the elephant's back. "Hello!"

"Hello yourself!" answered Tum Tum, and his voice was deep and rumbling, away down in his long nose or trunk, while Mappo's was chattery and shrill, as a monkey's voice always is.

"Well, where did you come from?" asked Mappo. "I've often seen you, or some elephant friends of yours in the jungle. How did you get on this ship with the other animals? You don't mean to say that the hunter men caught you—you, a great big strong elephant, do you?"

"That's just what they did, Mappo," said Tum Tum, and the sailor, looking at the two animals, did not know they were telling secrets to each other.

"I'll just leave 'em together a while," said the sailor. "I don't believe the monkey will run away, and, as he's getting homesick, it may make him feel better to be with the elephant a while."

Mappo was indeed getting homesick for the jungle, and for his folks, but when he saw Tum Tum, he felt much better.

"How did they catch you?" asked the monkey, as the sailor went up on deck, while Mappo and the elephant stayed down in the lower part of the ship, where it was nice and warm, talking to one another.

"Oh, the hunters made a big, strong fence in the jungle," said Tum Tum. "They left one opening in it, and then they began to drive us elephants along toward it. We did not know what was happening until it was too late, and at last we were caught fast in a sort of big trap, and could not get out."

"I should think you were so strong that you could easily have gotten out," Mappo said.

"Well, we did try—we wild elephants," spoke Tum Tum. "We rushed at the bamboo fence, and tried to break it down with our big heads. But tame elephants, who had helped to drive us into the trap, came up, and struck us with their trunks, and stuck us with their tusks, and told us to be good, and not to break the fence, and that we would be kindly treated. So we behaved, and, after a while, we found ourselves on this ship."

"Do you like it here?" asked Mappo.

"Well, it isn't so bad," said Tum Tum. "I get all I want to eat, and I don't have to hunt for it. I am to go in a circus and menagerie, I hear. I don't quite know what that is, do you?"

"Not exactly," answered Mappo, scratching his nose.

"Well, maybe we'll be in it together," went on Tum Tum. "But how did you happen to get caught, and brought away from the jungle, little monkey?"

Then Mappo told of being caught in the net when he picked up the pieces of cocoanut.

"Were any other animals caught with you?" asked Tum Tum.

"Oh, yes, the hunters had other animals—some monkeys, and a big tiger in a cage. He was named Sharp-Tooth, the tiger was."

"Hush!" whispered Tum Tum through his trunk, and looking around carefully, he went on: "Don't let him know I'm here!"

"Let who know?" asked Mappo.

"Sharp-Tooth, the tiger. Don't tell him I'm here," Tum Tum said.

"Why not?" the little monkey wanted to know.

"Well, because he and I aren't friends," said Tum Tum. "You know in the jungle, hunters sometimes ride on the backs of myself, and my elephant friends, to hunt tigers. That's why the tigers don't like us. So don't mention to Sharp-Tooth that I'm on board this ship."

"I won't, of course," spoke Mappo in his funny, monkey talk. "But it wouldn't matter, anyhow, as he's in a cage."

"He might break loose, and scratch me," said Tum Tum. "So don't mention it to him."

Mappo promised not to. He sat up there on the elephant's back a long time, and they talked of many things that had happened in the jungle woods.

"Well, you two seem to like each other so well that I guess I'll leave you together," said the sailor, when he came back and found Mappo asleep on Tum Tum's back. "I'll bring the monkey's cage down here," the sailor went on, "and let him stay. They might just as well get acquainted, for they'll be together in the circus, anyhow."

"That will be nice," thought Mappo, as he heard what the sailor said.

Many things happened to Mappo aboard the ship in which he journeyed from the jungle to this country. I have not room to tell you about all of them in this book.

Once there came a great storm, so that the big ship rolled and rocked like a rocking-chair, and Mappo felt ill. So did Tum Tum, and the other elephants, and they made loud noises through their trunks. Mappo and the other monkeys chattered with fear, and even Sharp-Tooth, the big striped tiger, in his cage, was afraid, and growled, while the lions roared like thunder.

But finally the storm passed, the sea grew calm and the animals felt better. Then came a day when Mappo was shut up in his cage again. Most of the time he had been loose, to run about as he pleased.

"I'm sorry to have to do it, old chap," said his sailor friend, "but all you animals are going to be taken off the ship now, and put ashore, and we don't want to lose you."

"I don't want to get lost, either," said Mappo to himself. "I wonder what is going to happen now."

Many things happened to him, and also to Tum Tum and the others. Mappo's cage, as well as the cages holding the lions and tigers, were lifted off the ship onto land. Then they were put on big wagons and carted off through a strange place. At first Mappo thought it was a new kind of jungle, for he saw some trees.

But when Mappo saw many boys and girls, and men and women, all in strange dresses, not at all like the brown natives, and when he saw many houses, he knew it could not be a jungle. No, it was a big city where Mappo had been taken. And it was the city where the circus stayed in winter, the animals living in barns, and in menageries, instead of in tents. But when the warm summer came, they would be taken out on the road, and sent from place to place with the traveling circus. Of course, Mappo knew nothing of this yet. Neither did Tum Tum.

Mappo's cage, with a number of others, was finally put into a big barn, where it was nice and warm. On the earth-floor of the barn was sawdust, and Mappo saw many men and horses, and many strange things. Finally a man came up to Mappo's cage.

"Ha! So these are some of the monkeys I am to teach to do tricks, eh?" said the man. "Well, they look like nice monkeys. And that one seems a little tame. I think I'll begin on him," and he pointed right at Mappo.

"Better look out," said another man. "Maybe he is an ugly chap, and will bite you."

"Oh, indeed I won't!" chattered Mappo. "I guess I know better than that!" But of course the circus man did not understand this monkey talk. Mappo jumped about in his cage, for he felt that he was going to be taken out, and he was tired of being shut up. He wanted to hang by his tail, and do other things, as he had done in the jungle.

"He's a lively little fellow, anyhow," said the circus man, as he opened the door of Mappo's cage. "Come on out, old chap," he went on, "and let's see what you look like."

Very gently he took Mappo out, and Mappo was very quiet. He wanted to show the man how polite and nice even a jungle monkey could be, when he tried.

"You're a nice fellow," the man said, stroking Mappo's back. "Now let's see. I guess I'll teach you first to ride a pony, or a dog, and then jump through paper hoops. After that you can turn somersaults, and sit up at the table and eat like a real child. Oh, I'll teach you many tricks."

Mappo did not understand very much of this talk. No monkey could. But Mappo did understand the word "eat," and he wondered when the man was going to feed him, for Mappo was hungry.

All around the circus barn different animals were being taught tricks, for the men were training them to be ready for the summer circus in the big tents. Horses were racing about sawdust rings, men were shouting and calling, and snapping long whips. In one corner a man was trying to make an elephant stand on his hind legs. Mappo looked a second time.

"Why, that's Tum Tum! He's learning tricks too!" said Mappo, to himself. "That's fine! I hope he and I can do tricks together."

Tum Tum did not look very happy. A long rope was fastened to him, and he was being pulled up so his head and trunk were in the air. That's how elephants are first taught to do the trick of standing on their hind legs. After a bit they learn to do it without being hoisted up by a rope.

"Now then, monkey boy, here we are!" exclaimed the man who had taken Mappo out of his cage. The man soon found that Mappo was good and gentle. "Now for your first trick," the man said. "Here, Prince!"

A great big, shaggy dog, almost as large as Sharp-Tooth, the tiger, came bounding into the circus ring. Right at Mappo rushed the dog, barking as loudly as he could:

"Bow wow! Bow wow! Bow wow!"

CHAPTER VIII

MAPPO AND HIS TRICKS

Mappo, the merry monkey, gave one look at the big dog rushing at him, and then, with a chatter of fright, sprang right up on the shoulder of the circus man. There Mappo sat, shivering, and looking down at the dog who kept on barking.

"Oh ho! So you're afraid, are you?" asked the man, as he put up his hand and patted Mappo. "Well, you don't need to be, little chap. Prince wouldn't hurt you a bit, would you, old chap?"

"Bow wow!" barked the dog, and I think he meant that he certainly would not—that he loved monkeys. In fact, any one would have loved Mappo, he was so kind and gentle, even though he had not had much training.

"Now, Prince, just show this monkey how you can stand on your head," went on the circus man. "Show him how it's done."

The dog kicked his hind legs up in the air, and there he was, standing up partly on his head, and partly on his forepaws.

"That'll do, Prince!" the man called. "Down!"

"Bow wow!" barked Prince, as he turned a somersault, and stood on his four feet.

"You'll soon be doing tricks like that, little monkey," went on the circus man, speaking to Mappo, as though the little chap from the jungle could understand and answer him.

And, as I have told you, Mappo could understand pretty nearly all the man said, but he could not talk back to him, except in monkey language, and that the man did not understand.

"Now, Prince," said the circus man, "Mappo is going to have a ride on your back. I want you to go slowly with him at first so he will not fall off. Later on, you may run fast, and we'll have a race, with other monkeys on the backs of other dogs. And, when Mappo has learned to ride dog-back, I'll teach him to ride pony-back."

"Bow wow!" barked Prince, just as though he understood it all.

A bright red blanket was strapped around Prince, like a saddle on a horse, and over the dog's head were put some straps like the reins of a horse. Those were for Mappo to take hold of, and pretend he was driving the dog around the ring.

"All right now. Here we go!" cried the man. "Come, Mappo!"

Mappo, who had been watching Tum Tum learn to stand on his hind legs, now looked at the man and dog. The man lifted up the monkey and set him on the dog's back. He also put the reins in Mappo's little paws.

"Now go, Prince!" said the man, and he walked along with the dog, holding Mappo on the back of Prince.

At first Mappo did not understand what was wanted of him, and when Prince started off, the little monkey grew afraid, and tried to jump down and run away. But the man spoke gently to him.

"There now, old fellow," said the circus man kindly. "No one is going to hurt you. You'll be all right. Just sit on. Prince won't run away with you."

Mappo was not so frightened now, and as the man held him on the dog's back, he did not fall off. Around and around in a ring went Prince carrying Mappo. Finally the monkey saw that he was in no danger of falling, and he sat up straighter.

"I guess you can go alone now," said the man. "Go on, Prince!"

Mappo sat up proudly, holding the reins. He was riding alone, though of course not very fast, for Prince only walked now.

For two or three days Mappo practiced this trick, and each day he did it better. Each day, too, when he had finished it, he was given something good to eat, and so was Prince.

"Now we'll try it faster to-day," said the man, after Mappo had been in the circus about a week. "Run, Prince, and give Mappo a fast ride."

Off started Prince, almost before Mappo was ready for him. And, just as you might expect, Mappo fell off and rolled over and over in the sawdust.

"Chatter-chatter-chat! Bur-r-r-r! Buz-z-z-z! Wur-r-r-r-r!" went Mappo, excitedly.

"Bow wow!" barked Prince, capering about.

"Hold on! That's not the way to do it! You must hold on tightly!" cried the circus man.

"Did you hurt yourself, Mappo?" asked Tum Tum, the jolly elephant, who was resting, after having stood up on his hind legs. He had seen Mappo fall.

"No," answered the monkey, "I didn't hurt myself, but I don't like to fall that way. I don't like that trick."

"Never mind," spoke Tum Tum kindly. "The next time you do it, and Prince runs fast, just wrap your tail around him, as you used to wrap it around a tree limb in the big jungle. Then you won't fall."

"That's a good idea—I'll do it!" cried Mappo.

"Now we'll try it again," said the circus man. "Go a bit slower this time, Prince."

"Bow wow! I will!" barked the dog.

Once more Mappo took his place on the red blanket on the dog's back. He took the reins in his little paws, that were almost like your hands, and then, remembering what Tum Tum had said to him, Mappo wound his tail around the neck of Prince, but not so tightly as to hurt him.

"Bow wow! What are you doing that for?" asked the dog. He knew how to speak so Mappo would understand him.

"I am doing it so I will not fall off when you run fast, Prince," answered Mappo.

"Ha! Ha! Very good!" laughed Prince, in the only way dogs can laugh, which is by barking softly. "That's a good trick, little monkey. If other monkeys were as smart as you they would learn their lessons more quickly. Now hold on tight, for I am going to run!"

"I will!" promised Mappo.

The circus man looked at what Mappo had done.

"That is a smart little monkey," he said. "Now he will not fall."

And this time, when Prince started off, and ran very fast around the sawdust ring, Mappo did not fall off. His tail, which was as good as a hand to him, was wrapped about the neck of Prince, and kept Mappo from slipping.

Mappo could now do the dog-riding trick very well. No matter how fast Prince ran, the monkey would not fall off. A few days later more dogs and other monkeys were brought into the circus ring in the big barn, and they, too, raced around. But none of them could go as fast as Mappo and Prince, and, each time, they won the race around the sawdust ring.

"That certainly is a smart little monkey!" the circus man would say over and over again. "I shall teach him many tricks. I will now see how he can ride on the back of a pony, and, after that, I will teach him to jump through paper hoops."

Mappo did not very well understand what this meant, but he made up his mind he would do whatever was asked of him, and that he would do it as well as he could.

A few days later some little Shetland ponies were brought into the barn, and Mappo was placed on the back of one of them. The pony was a little larger than Prince, and Mappo was farther from the ground. But the little monkey had climbed tall trees in the jungle, and he was not afraid of going up even on an elephant's back. So, of course, he was not afraid on Trotter, the pony.

A blanket was strapped on Trotter's back, and as there was an iron ring in the strap, Mappo stuck his tail through that, and so held on. The other monkeys, who were also to ride ponies, saw what Mappo was doing, and they did the same thing.

"Ha! It's good to have a smart monkey in the circus," said the man. "He shows the others what to do."

Mappo was so smart, and such a good rider, that he easily took the lead in the race, and kept it. The ponies ran faster than the dogs had done, but, even then, neither Mappo nor any of the other monkeys fell off, for their tails were in the iron rings of the straps.

"Well, how are you coming on?" asked Tum Tum of Mappo one day, when they were resting after having eaten their dinners.

"Fine!" answered Mappo. "I can do many tricks now. What are you learning?"

"Oh, many things," answered Tum Tum. "I have to play ball, grind a hand-organ with my trunk and make music, I have to play soldier, march around, and stand up on my hind legs and on my head."

"Is it hard work?" asked Mappo.

"Yes, but I like it," said Tum Tum. And some day soon, in another book, I shall tell you the many adventures of Tum Tum, the jolly elephant.

"Well, now for a new trick," said the circus man to Mappo, one morning. "Soon it will be time for the circus to go out on the road, under the big tents, and I want you to do many tricks for the boys and girls."

"I'll do all I can!" chattered Mappo, in his monkey language.

This time, after he had ridden around the ring once or twice on the back of Prince, the circus man brought out some big wooden hoops, covered with paper.

"You are to jump through these, Mappo," said the man. "Come, let me see how you can do it." Mappo was riding on Prince's back. All of a sudden, as Prince went around the sawdust ring, he came near to one of the rings the man held out. Mappo did not in the least know what he was to do, but, all at once, the man caught him up off the dog's back, and fairly tossed him through the paper ring. The paper burst with a crackling noise, and Mappo felt himself falling.

"Oh dear!" thought the little monkey, "I wonder where I shall land!"

CHAPTER IX

MAPPO RUNS AWAY

Mappo was so surprised, as he felt himself fairly flying through the paper hoop, that he did not know exactly what was happening.

"I may land on the back of Tum Tum, for all I know," he thought.

But, just as he said that to himself, he came down on the back of Prince, as if nothing had happened.

"Hello, here we are again!" cried Prince, running on around the sawdust ring, with Mappo on his back. "You did that trick all right."

"Yes, but the man tossed me through the paper-covered hoop," spoke Mappo, wonderingly.

"That was to show you how to do it," went on Prince. "I have seen many monkeys do that trick."

"Oh, I see," said Mappo. "There's the man with another hoop. Shall I jump right through it?"

"Yes, don't wait for him to toss you," Prince said. "Though he didn't hurt you, did he?"

"Not a bit," laughed Mappo, who rather liked doing that trick.

The circus man stood up on a little box, holding the ring, all covered with red paper, ready for Mappo to jump through. And the man would have picked Mappo up, and tossed him through the ring, only the monkey did not wait for that. Instead, he gave a jump himself, and right through the ring he went, coming down on Prince's back as nicely as you please. Prince kept right on running around the sawdust ring.

"Fine! That's the way to do it!" cried the circus man, clapping his hands. "I'll have to get you to show the other monkeys how to do it, Mappo! You're the first monkey who ever learned that trick so quickly."

I guess I told you Mappo was a smart little chap.

The rest of that day he spent practicing jumping through more paper-covered hoops, doing some of his jumps from the back of Trotter, the pony. Then other monkeys were brought in, and they watched Mappo.

"Now let's see if they can do it," said the man, after Mappo had done his trick several times. Well, the other monkeys tried, and while some of them could do it pretty well, others fell off, or else were afraid of the paper hoops. No one did it as well as Mappo.

From then on, the little monkey learned many circus tricks. He did not learn all of them as easily as he had learned to ride the dog and pony, or jump through the hoops. In fact, it took him several days to learn the trick of turning a somersault. And it took him longer to learn to sit up at a table, and eat with a knife, fork and spoon, dressed up like a little boy, with real clothes on.

All this while the circus animals had remained in the big, warm barn, for it was still winter. But spring and summer were coming, and would soon be over all the land. Then the circus would start out with the tents, and the big red, green and golden wagons.

Other animals were being trained, too. Tum Tum, the jolly elephant could do many tricks, and Mappo loved to watch his big friend, with the long trunk, and the long white teeth, or tusks, sticking out of his mouth. Tum Tum's trainer would sometimes sit on these tusks, or on Tum Tum's trunk, and ride around the ring. Tum Tum liked his keeper, or trainer, very much, just as Mappo liked his own circus man.

One day, when Mappo had finished doing his tricks for the day, and had been given a whole, ripe, yellow banana for himself, as a treat for being good and smart, the little monkey wandered off to another part of the circus barn. Mappo, unlike the other monkeys, was not kept in a cage, or chained up.

As Mappo was walking along he came underneath a cage, and from over his head came a loud roar.

"A lion!" cried Mappo, springing away. "He'll get me!"

In the jungle he and his brothers and sisters had been taught to run and hide when a lion roared, and, for the moment, Mappo did just as he had been used to doing in the jungle. Then he sort of laughed to himself, in a way monkeys have, and he said:

"Ha! Ha! That lion can't get at me! He is locked in his cage. I'm not afraid."

But, just the same, Mappo ran over on the other side of the circus barn, and watched the lion from there.

The "King of Beasts," as he is called, though a lion is often no braver that any other animal, paced back and forth in his cage. He peered out between the bars, and tried to break them with his big paws. But he could not. Now and then the lion would utter a deep, loud roar, that seemed to shake the very ground. I suppose he roared as he had done in the jungle, when he wanted to let the other animals know he was coming. A lion must be very proud of his roar.

"Well, you can't get me, anyhow," thought Mappo. "You are safe in your cage, and I am glad of it."

"Well, how are you to-day, Tum Tum?" asked Mappo, of the jolly elephant.

"Tired. Very tired!" exclaimed Tum Tum.

"What makes you tired?" asked the monkey.

"Doing so many tricks," the elephant answered. "And you know I am a big, heavy chap, and it tires me to run fast around the ring. But never mind, we will soon be out of here, and on a journey."

"Where are we going?" asked Mappo.

"To travel from town to town, as all circuses do. We shall soon be living in tents," the elephant answered.

"I'll like that," said Mappo. "I am getting rather tired of staying here so long."

And, surely enough, a few days later, the circus started out "on the road," as it is called. The big red, golden and green wagons were drawn by many horses, and rumbled up hill and down. In the wagons the animals and tents and other things, all of which go to make up a circus, were carried.

One day, after a lot of traveling, part of which was by train, Mappo and the other animals came to a place where a big, white tent was set up in a wide, green field. The tent had been set up in the night, ready for the circus.

"Ah! Now our real circus work will begin!" said Tum Tum. And so it did.

The bands began to play, and when the tent was filled with boys and girls, and their papas and mammas, and grandpas and grandmas, there was a grand procession of all the performers. The elephants, of which Tum Tum was one, also marched around, as did lots of the ponies and dogs.

"I wonder when it will come my turn to do tricks?" thought Mappo. His turn soon came. The kind circus man who had taught the little monkey, came and dressed him up in a nice red suit, with a little red cap. Then Prince, the dog, was led in, wearing a fine yellow blanket.

"Now for the race!" cried the man, as Mappo jumped up on Prince's back. The other monkeys jumped up on the backs of other dogs, and, as the band played, off they ran.

Mappo liked it very much, especially when the children laughed and clapped their hands, for he was glad he had pleased them. Faster and faster went the racing dogs, and Mappo and Prince won.

Then came the jumping through the paper hoops, first from the backs of dogs, and, afterward backs of the ponies. In all of these tricks Mappo did very well.

Then Mappo did his other tricks—turning somersaults, standing on his head, and even riding a little bicycle the man had made for him. That was Mappo's best trick, and one that ended his part of the circus. He rode around a little wooden platform on the bicycle, holding a flag over his shoulder, and my! how the children did laugh at that.

Mappo did not see all the circus. As soon as his act was over, he was taken back to his cage, but he was not chained up. His keeper knew he could trust Mappo not to run away.

Mappo wandered around the animal tent. After a while he came to where the tiger's cage stood.

"Ah ha! There you are!" snarled Sharp-Tooth, the striped tiger, as he saw Mappo. "You're the monkey who is to blame for my being here."

"I to blame! How?" asked Mappo.

"Yes, you are to blame," went on Sharp-Tooth. "You wouldn't open my cage, and let me out when we were in the jungle. Never mind! I'll fix you! When I get out of here—and some day I'm going to break loose—when I get out of here, I'll bite you."

"Oh dear!" thought Mappo. "I hope that never happens!" and he went off to talk to Tum Tum, the jolly elephant.

For nearly a week the circus traveled from town to town, Mappo doing his tricks very well indeed. Once again Sharp-Tooth, the tiger, said to the monkey chap:

"Oh, wait until I get hold of you. I was nearly out of my cage last night. To-night I'll be out for sure, and then I'll fix you!"

Poor Mappo was frightened. The more he thought of the tiger getting loose and biting him, the more frightened he became. And that day, as Mappo was riding along in his own cage in the circus wagon, he thought he heard the tiger getting loose from the big cage.

"Oh, he'll get me, sure!" cried Mappo. He looked up. The door of his cage was open the least little bit. Mappo pulled it open wider with his paws, and then, when none of the circus men was looking, Mappo slipped out, and dropped down to the road.

The door of his cage snapped shut after Mappo got out, keeping the other monkeys in.

"I'm going to run away," said Mappo. "I'm not going to stay, and let that bad tiger catch me." And so Mappo ran away.

CHAPTER X

MAPPO AND SQUINTY

Mappo, as soon as he got outside the traveling circus cage on wheels, looked all about him to see if any one were watching him. But no one seemed to be doing so.

His man friend, who had trained him to do many tricks, was riding on the seat with the driver of the big monkey-cage wagon, and this man never looked around, as Mappo slipped out. All the other circus men were too busy to look after one monkey.

Mappo slipped down to the dusty country road, along which the circus procession was then going, and quickly running across it, the merry little monkey hid in the bushes on the other side.

Slowly the big circus wagons rumbled past the place where Mappo was hiding in the bushes. When the cage, in which Sharp-Tooth, the tiger, was pacing up and down, came along, the big striped beast growled and roared, and to Mappo it sounded just as if he were saying:

"Where's that monkey? Oh, wait until I get hold of him! He wouldn't let me out of my cage, and I'll fix him!"

When the last wagon in, the procession had gone past—and it was the steam piano which brought up at the end—Mappo breathed a long breath.

"Now I'm all right!" he thought. "They can't find me now. I'm going over into those woods. Maybe there is a jungle where I can find cocoanuts."

Scrambling over rocks, stones and fences, Mappo made his way to the big woods. It looked cool and green there, much better than the hot, dusty road, down which the circus procession was rumbling, with the big red, green and gold wagons.

Mappo was much disappointed when he reached the woods. He could not see any cocoanuts or bananas, and those were the things he liked best of all.

"I wonder what I shall eat," said Mappo, for he was quite hungry.

He ran about, climbing trees, going away up to the top, and hanging down by his tail. He had not had a chance to do this since he had been with the circus, and, really, it was lots of fun for him.

Soon he felt hungry again, and he looked around for something to chew. He saw nothing.

"Oh dear!" he cried out loud. "I wonder what I can eat."

"Ha!" cried a grunting little voice near him, "why don't you eat acorns, as I do?"

"What's that? Who are you? Where are you?" asked Mappo, looking up and down.

"Here I am, under this bush," the voice went on, and out walked a little pig.

"What's your name?" asked Mappo.

"My name is Squinty," answered the little pig. I suppose you had guessed that before I told you—at least those of you who have read my other book, called "Squinty, the Comical Pig."

"Squinty, eh?" remarked Mappo. "That's a queer name."

"They call me that because one of my eyes squints," said the little pig. "See!" and he looked up at Mappo in such a funny way, with one eye half shut, and the other wide open, and with one ear cocked forward and the other backward, that Mappo had to laugh.

"My name is Mappo, and I'm from the circus. I've run away, and I'm hungry," the monkey said.

"Ha! I'm running away myself," said Squinty, "and I was hungry too, but I found some acorns to eat."

"What are acorns, and where did you run from?" asked Mappo.

"Acorns are nuts, good for pigs to eat," Squinty answered, "and I ran away from my pen."

"I wish I had something to eat," said Mappo. "I am very hungry."

"Come with me, and I'll see if I can't find you something to eat," Squinty said. "Then you can tell me all about the circus, and I'll tell you all about my pen."

"All right," agreed Mappo, and the two little animal friends went off together into the woods.

"Are there any cocoanuts here?" asked Mappo, when they had gone on for some distance.

"I don't know," answered Squinty. "What are cocoanuts?"

Mappo told the little pig how cocoanuts and bananas grew in the jungle, and the little pig told about how he liked sour milk and things like that. And, after a while, they managed to find some berries for Mappo to eat, as he did not like the acorn nuts.

The two friends went on in the woods for some distance, and they were having a good time, telling each other about their adventures, when, all of a sudden, as Mappo was swinging along by his tail on a tree branch, he stopped short and cried:

"Ha! They're after me. I guess I'd better run."

"Who is after you?" asked Squinty.

"The circus men. They must have found out I ran away."

Mappo and Squinty looked through the bushes, and they saw a number of men in red coats and blue trousers coming through the woods. Squinty also saw something else.

"Oh, look!" cried the little pig. "What is that funny animal with two tails? I'm afraid of him, he's so big!"

Mappo looked and laughed.

"He hasn't two tails," he said. "One is his tail and the other is his trunk. That is Tum Tum, the circus elephant. And you needn't be afraid of him, for he is the jolliest elephant in the whole show.

"But I'm not going to be caught," went on Mappo. "I want to run away farther, and have more adventures. So I guess I'll go before Tum Tum and the men see me. Good-by, Squinty. I'm glad I met you."

"And I'm glad that I met you," said the comical little pig. Then he ran one way through the woods, for he did not want to be caught, either, and Mappo ran the other way.

On and on through the woods roamed the merry little monkey, and many things happened to him. He met Slicko, the jumping girl squirrel, and in the book about Slicko you may read all about her wonderful adventures.

At first Mappo had lots of fun, after running away from the circus. It was warm, and he managed to make himself a little house of leaves, in the woods where he slept nights, or when it rained. But, for all that, he did not have as good things to eat as he had had when he was in his cage. He missed doing his tricks, too, and he missed seeing the boys and girls and their parents, in the big tent.

One day, as Mappo was asleep in the woods, he was suddenly awakened by feeling himself caught by two hands, and a voice cried:

"Oh, I've caught a monkey. I'm going to take him home and keep him. Oh, a real, live monkey!"

Mappo opened his eyes, and he saw that a boy was holding him, and holding him so tightly that the little monkey could not get away.

"Well, I'm caught!" thought Mappo, but he was not very sorry.

CHAPTER XI

MAPPO AND THE ORGAN-MAN

Some monkeys, if they had been caught by a boy, in the woods, would have bit and scratched and fought to get away. But Mappo was both a merry monkey, and a good, kind one. So, when he saw that the boy was holding him tightly, Mappo made up his mind that it would not be nice to try to get away.

Besides, he liked boys, as well as girls, for so many of them had fed him peanuts in the circus. And I rather think that Mappo was getting tired of having run away, for he did not find these woods as nice as he thought he would.

"Oh, father, look!" the boy cried. "I've caught a monkey."

"Have you, really?" asked a man, who came up near the boy. "Why, so you have!" he exclaimed. "It must have escaped from the circus that went through here the other day."

"Oh, father, mayn't we keep it?" the boy asked, as he patted Mappo. "See, he is real tame, and maybe he does tricks."

"Of course I'm tame and do tricks!" Mappo chattered, but the boy did not understand monkey talk.

"Oh, let me keep him!" the boy begged of his father.

"Well, I don't know," spoke the man, slowly. "A monkey is a queer sort of a pet, and we haven't really any place for him."

"Oh, I'll make a place," the boy said. "Do let me keep him!"

"Well, you may try," his father said. "But if the circus men come back after him, you'll have to give up your monkey. And he may run away, no matter what sort of a cage you keep him in."

"Oh, I don't believe he will," the boy said.

So Mappo was taken home to the boy's house. It was quite different from the circus where the merry little monkey had lived so long. There were no sawdust rings, no horses or other animals, and there was no performance in the afternoon, and none in the evening.

But, for all that, Mappo liked it. For one thing he got enough to eat, and the things he liked—cocoanuts and bananas, for the boy read in a book what monkeys liked, and got them for his new pet. The boy made a nice box cage for Mappo to sleep in, and tied him fast with a string around the collar, which Mappo wore.

"But I could easily loosen that string and get away if I wanted to," Mappo thought as he played with the knot in his odd little fingers. Monkeys can untie most knots, and a chain is about the only thing that will hold them.

The boy's mother was afraid of Mappo at first, but the little monkey was so kind and gentle, that she grew to like him. And Mappo was a very good monkey. He did not bite or scratch.

The house where the boy lived was quite different from the circus tent, or the big barn where Mappo had first learned to do tricks. There was an upstairs and downstairs to the house, and many windows. Mappo soon learned to go up and down stairs very well indeed, and he liked nothing better than to slide down the banisters. Sometimes he would climb up on the gas chandelier and hang by his tail. This always made the boy laugh.

"See, my monkey can do tricks!" he would cry.

Then, one day, something sad happened. Mappo was sitting near the dining-room window, which was open, and he was half asleep, for the sun was very warm. The little monkey was dreaming, perhaps of the days when he used to sleep in the tree-house in the jungle, or he may have been thinking of the time when he went with the circus.

Suddenly he was awakened by hearing some music. He looked out in the street, and there he saw a hand-organ man grinding away at the crank which made the nice music. Mappo liked it very much. It reminded him a little of the circus music.

And, as soon as the hand-organ man saw the monkey, he cried out:

"Ha! A monkey! Just what I need. My monkey has gone away, and I'll take this new little monkey to go around with me and get the pennies in his cap."

Then, before Mappo knew what was going to happen, the hand-organ man ran up to the open window, grabbed the little monkey off the sill, and, stuffing him under his coat, ran away down the street with him as fast as he could go.

"Let me go! Let me out!" chattered Mappo, in his own, queer language. The man paid no attention to him. Perhaps he did not understand what Mappo meant, though hand-organ men ought to know monkey talk, if any one does. At any rate, the man did not let Mappo go. Instead, he carried him on and on through the streets, until he came to the place where he lived.

"Now I'll put a chain and a long string on you, and take you around with me when I make music," said the hand-organ man. "You will have a little red cap to take the pennies the children give you."

While he was thus talking the man thrust Mappo into a box, that was not very clean, and tossed him a crust of bread.

"I wonder if that is all I am to get to eat," thought Mappo. "Oh, dear! I might better have stayed in the circus. It was nice at the boy's house, but it is not nice here."

Mappo was shut up in the box, with only a little water, and that one piece of bread crust to eat. And then the hand-organ man went to sleep.

Poor Mappo did not like this at all, but what could he do? He was shut up in a box, and try as he did, he could not get out. Some other monkey had lived in the box before. Mappo could tell that, because there were scratches and teeth marks in the wood which Mappo knew must have been made by some such little monkey as himself.

Mappo's life from then on, for some time, was rather hard. The next morning the hand-organ man fastened a chain to the collar of the monkey, and a long rope to the chain.

"Now I'll teach you to climb up on porch houses, go up the rain-water pipes, and up to windows, to get pennies," said the hand-organ man. "Come, be lively!"

He did not-have to teach Mappo very much, for the monkey could already do those things.

"Ha! I see you are a trick monkey!" the man said. "So much the better for me. I'll get many pennies from the children."

Then, every day, Mappo was made to go out with the man and his hand-organ, and when the man played tunes, Mappo would watch the windows of the houses in front of which his master stopped. The children would come to the windows when they heard the music.

"Go up and get the pennies!" the man would cry, and he would pull and jerk on the long string so that the collar around Mappo's neck choked and hurt him. Then the monkey would squeal, and hold the chain with his paw, so the pulling on it would not pain him so much. The hand-organ man was not very kind to Mappo.

But Mappo made up his mind he would do his best to please his master.

"Some day I may get loose," Mappo thought. "If I do, I'll run back to the circus, and never go away from it again. Oh that circus! And Tum Tum! I wonder if I'll ever see the jolly elephant again."

Thinking such thoughts as these, Mappo would climb up the front of the houses, to the windows, scrambling up the rain-water pipe, and he would take off his cap, and catch in it the pennies the children threw to him. Then sometimes, on the porch roof, Mappo would turn a somersault, or play soldier, doing some of his circus tricks. This made the children laugh again, and they would ask their mammas for more pennies.

"Ah, he is a fine monkey!" the hand-organ man would say. "He brings me much money."

The hand-organ man never let him loose; always was there that chain and string fast to the collar on Mappo's neck.

Mappo was made to wear a little red jacket, as well as a cap, and, as the things had been made for a smaller monkey than he, they were rather tight for him.

For many weeks Mappo was kept by the hand-organ man, and made to gather pennies. Mappo grew very tired of it.

"Oh, if I had only stayed with the circus," thought Mappo, sorrowfully.

One morning the hand-organ man got up earlier than usual.

"We make much money to-day," he said to Mappo, for he had a habit of speaking to the monkey as though he could understand. And indeed, Mappo knew a great deal of what his master said. "We will make many pennies to-day," went on the man. "Out by the big show, where everybody will be jolly."

He brushed Mappo's jacket and cap, and then, after a very little breakfast, out they started. Through street after street they went, but the man did not stop to play in front of any houses.

"I wonder why that is," thought Mappo, for his master had never done that before.

And then, all of a sudden, Mappo saw a big white tent, with gay flags flying from the poles. He saw the big red, gold and green wagons. He heard the neighing of the horses, the trumpeting of the elephants, the roaring of the lions, and the snarling of the tigers.

"Oh, it's the circus! It's my circus!" cried Mappo to himself, and so it was.

"Now we make much money!" said the hand-organ man. "The people who come to the circus have many pennies. They give them to me when I play. Come, Mappo, be lively—do tricks and get the pennies," and he shook the string and chain, hurting Mappo's neck.

Then the organ began to play. But Mappo did not hear it. He heard only the circus band. And he smelled the sawdust ring.

"Oh, I must get back to my dear circus!" he chattered. Then, with one big, strong pull of his paws, Mappo broke the collar around his neck, and, as fast as he could run, he scampered toward the big tent—the tent where he knew his cage was. Oh, how Mappo ran!

CHAPTER XII

MAPPO AND THE BABY

"Come back here! Come back! My monkey! He is running away!" cried the hand-organ man, as he raced after Mappo. Mappo looked behind, and saw his unkind master coming, so the little monkey ran faster than ever.

"Oh, if I can only find Tum Tum, the jolly elephant, and get up on his back, that man can never get me again!" thought Mappo. "I must find Tum Tum!"

Into the big circus tent ran Mappo. The show had not yet begun, and one of the men who was at the entrance to take tickets seeing Mappo, cried out:

"Ha! One of our monkeys must have gotten loose. I will call the animal trainer."

So Mappo came back to the circus again. But his adventures were not yet over.

That afternoon, when he had been given his own circus suit, which fitted him better than the one the hand-organ man had put on him, Mappo went through his tricks in the big tent. He had not forgotten them.

He rode on the back of Prince, the big dog, and also on Trotter, the pony, coming in first in every race. Then Mappo jumped through the paper-covered hoops, he played soldier, and he sat up at the table and ate his dinner with a knife, fork and spoon, almost as nicely as you could have done it. He used his napkin, too.

The circus traveled on and on. One day it came to a big city, and some of the tents were set up in a field, near some houses. From his place near his cage Mappo could look out of the crack in the top of the tent, and see the windows of the houses near him.

"I used to climb in windows like that," said Mappo to Tum Tum. "I used to go up the rain-water pipe to get the pennies from the children."

"It must have been fun for you," said Tum Tum, "as you are such a good climber."

"Oh, it wasn't so much fun as you'd imagine," answered Mappo as he slyly tickled another monkey with a straw. Mappo was always up to some trick or other; he was a very merry monkey.

It was almost time for the circus performance to start. Mappo was thinking he had better go, and get on his pretty new red, white and blue suit, when suddenly, from outside the tent, he heard the cry of:

"Fire! Fire! Fire!"

Now Mappo knew what a fire was. There used to be a fire in the stove at the big circus barn, and once he went too close and burned his paw.

So Mappo knew what fire meant, even though it was cried in some other language than monkey talk. Then Mappo looked out of a crack in the tent, and he saw one of the houses, near the circus grounds, all ablaze. Black smoke was coming from it.

"One of those houses is burning," said Mappo to Tum Tum. The monkey had often seen the natives, in his jungle, kindle fires at night to cook their suppers, and also to keep wild beasts away. For wild beasts are afraid of fire.

"A house burning, eh?" said Tum Tum. "Well, that is nothing to us. We have to go on with the show, no matter what happens."

"I'm going out to see it," spoke Mappo. "I have a little time yet before I must do my tricks."

Mappo was not chained, so he had no trouble in slipping under the tent, and in going toward the burning house. There was great excitement. Men, boys, girls and women were running all around. Some of them were carrying things out of the blazing dwelling. Then up came the fire engines, tooting and whistling. Mappo of course did not know what fire engines were. All he cared for was the black smoke, and the bright, red fire.

Suddenly a woman in the crowd began to scream.

"My baby! Oh, my little baby is up in that room," and she pointed to one on the side of the house which was not yet burning as much as the rest. "Oh, my baby!" she cried, and she tried to run back into the blazing house, but some men stopped her.

"The firemen will get your baby," they said.

"Oh, they will never be in time!" the woman cried.

Just then Mappo's circus trainer came running up.

"Oh, here you are!" he cried to Mappo. "I was afraid you had run away again."

"No! No!" chattered Mappo, in his own language.

Mappo reached up, and put his arms around the keeper's neck. Just then the woman cried again:

"My baby! Oh, my baby is left behind in the room, and the stairs are all on fire. How can I get him?"

"What, is there a baby in the house?" cried Mappo's trainer.

"Yes. In that room where the window is," she said. "Oh, but we can't get him."

"Yes, I think we can!" said the circus man. "Mappo, my monkey is very strong, and he is a good climber. There is a rain-water pipe going up the side of the house, close to the window. I'll send my monkey up the pipe, and he can go in through the window, get the baby, and bring it down to you."

"Oh, a monkey could never do that!" sobbed the woman.

"Yes, my monkey can," the man replied. "Here, Mappo!" he called. "Up you go!" and he pointed to the rain-water pipe on the side of the house. "Go in the window and get the baby—get the little one and bring her safely down."

"Yes, yes!" chattered Mappo, only he spoke in his language and the man talked as we talk. But Mappo understood. Many times he had been sent up rain-water pipes by the hand-organ man. Of course this was a bit different, for this house was on fire. But there were not many flames on the side where the pipe was.

Mappo sprang for the pipe, and began to climb up it. He did not know exactly what he was going after, but he knew it must be something important, or his master would not be so excited.

"Get the baby! Get the baby!" cried the circus man, for the firemen had not yet come up with their ladders. Of course they could have saved the baby, if they had been in time. But it would soon be too late.

Up and up the rain-water pipe went the nimble Mappo. In a few seconds he was on the window sill of the room. He stood there, looking down at his master.

"Go on in! Get the baby and bring her down!" called the circus man, waving his arms at Mappo.

Down into the room jumped Mappo. He knew at once it was a bedroom, for he had been in such rooms in the home of the boy who found him in the woods. And, in a little bed, close to the window, was something that Mappo at first thought was a large doll, such as the sisters of the boy used to play with.

"I wonder if this is the baby," said Mappo. "I guess it is. I'll carry it down."

The baby was asleep. Mappo took her up in one of his strong hairy arms, and, very luckily he picked her right-side up. Some monkeys would carry a baby upside down, and think nothing of it. But Mappo was different.

With the baby held closely, the monkey jumped to the window sill again, and how his master and the others yelled when they saw him!

"He has her! Oh, he has your baby!" cried the circus man.

Down the rain-pipe came Mappo carrying the little baby, which was just beginning to wake up and cry. Mappo gave the little one to his master, who put the baby in its anxious mother's arms.

"There's your child," he said.

"Oh, what a smart monkey, to save her!" sobbed the woman, but her tears were tears of joy. Then the firemen put out the fire in the house, and no one was hurt. Mappo choked a little from the smoke, but he did not mind that.

"You surely are a smart monkey!" said the circus man, as he took him back to the tent to do his tricks. The show went on after a while, and Mappo was more looked at than any animal, for every one heard how he had saved the baby.

And, after the show was over that night, the father of the baby went to the circus man and said:

"I want to buy the monkey that saved my little girl. Please sell him to me. We will give him a good home, and we will always love him, for what he did for us."

"Well, I don't like to lose such a good trick monkey," said Mappo's master, "but I will let you have him. Be kind to him, for he is a good little chap."

"Oh, we'll be very kind to him," the baby's papa promised. "We have a dog named Don, and a cat named Tabby. I am sure Mappo will like them. We will be very good to him."

And so Mappo, after having lived in the jungle, and afterward joining a circus, went to live at the home of the baby, after it was built over, for it was badly damaged by the fire. And Mappo made friends with Don and Tabby and had a lovely time.

But there are other animals of whose lives I can tell you, and the next book in this series is going to be called "Tum Tum, the Jolly Elephant: His Many Adventures."

"Weren't you afraid when you climbed up that rain-water pipe to get the baby?" asked Don the dog of Mappo, one day.

"I wasn't afraid of climbing, but I was a little afraid of the fire," said the monkey.

"I wish I were as brave as you," said Tabby, the cat. "Come on, let's have a game of tag."

And the three animal friends played a game very much like our tag; and now we will say good-by to them.

THE END